This
PJ BOOK
belongs to

_____

_____

PJ Library®

JEWISH BEDTIME STORIES and SONGS

For my grandsons:
Darwin, Ari, and Levi,
with love.
—SES

To fifty years of joy and blessings:
My husband Jeff's fiftieth birthday, the Kellers' fiftieth wedding anniversary,
and the Rothenbergs' fiftieth wedding anniversary.
—JRK

The Shema in the Mezuzah: Listening to Each Other

2013 PJ Library Quality Paperback Edition, First Printing

For information regarding permission to reprint material from this book, please mail or fax your request in writing to Jewish Lights Publishing, Permissions Department, at the address / fax number listed below, or e-mail your request to permissions@jewishlights.com.

Library of Congress Cataloging-in-Publication Data
Sasso, Sandy Eisenberg.
  The Shema in the mezuzah : listening to each other / Sandy Eisenberg Sasso ; Illustrations by Joani Keller Rothenberg.
    p. cm.
  Summary: Grandma tells Annie a story to explain how, a long time ago, a wise rabbi settled an argument between two groups of townspeople who could not agree on how to hang a mezuzah.
  ISBN 978-1-58023-506-8
  [1. Mezuzah—Fiction. 2. Jews—Fiction. 3. Judaism—Customs and practices—Fiction. 4. Listening—Fiction.] I. Rothenberg, Joani, 1964– ill. II. Title.
  PZ7.S24914She 2012
  [E]—dc23
                              2012007709

10 9 8 7 6 5 4 3 2 1

Manufactured in China
Jacket and interior design: Heather Pelham

Published by Jewish Lights Publishing
A Division of Longhill Partners, Inc.
Sunset Farm Offices, Route 4, P.O. Box 237
Woodstock, VT 05091
Tel: (802) 457-4000   Fax: (802) 457-4004
www.jewishlights.com

The Shema in the Mezuzah

Listening to Each Other

Rabbi Sandy Eisenberg Sasso

Illustrations by Joani Keller Rothenberg

For People of All Faiths, All Backgrounds

JEWISH LIGHTS Publishing

Woodstock, Vermont

In the twelfth century, the great Torah commentator Rashi and his grandson, Rabbenu Tam, had a disagreement about how to place the mezuzah on the doorpost of the home. Rashi thought it should be placed vertically; Rabbenu Tam believed it should be in a horizontal position. As a compromise, it became the custom to put up the mezuzah slanted into the home.

nnie's grandmother had just moved into a new home. Annie was glad all the boxes were unpacked. Now her grandmother would have time to bake her favorite chocolate chip cookies.

"Can we bake now?" Annie asked expectantly.

"Not just yet!" her grandmother smiled. "There is still one more box to open."

Annie's grandmother carefully opened a small package that Annie recognized right away.

"That's a mezuzah. We have one on the doorway of our home," Annie exclaimed. "My mom told me that inside is special paper and on it are very important words, the words of the *Shema*."

Shema Yisrael:

Listen, Israel, the Eternal our God, the Eternal is One.
Speak these words when you go out and when you come in,
when you lie down and when you get up.

Annie watched as her grandmother said a blessing and put up the mezuzah on her doorway.

"Grandma, why doesn't the mezuzah stand up straight or lie down flat?" Annie asked. "Why does the mezuzah look like it's leaning to one side? It's the same way at my home."

Her grandmother smiled. "Let me tell you a story."

Once there was a town where many people had mezuzahs
but no one knew how to put them up.

   Perhaps there are instructions inside the mezuzah, the
townspeople thought. They looked at the special paper inside the
mezuzah. It contained words from the Torah but no instruction
on how to put the mezuzah on the doorpost.

5

Half the people said, "We should put the mezuzah standing up, since the words tell us to say the *Shema* when we get up in the morning."

Half the people insisted that the mezuzah should be lying down. "The words tell us to say the *Shema* when we lie down at night."

Neither side wanted to listen to the other. They just argued, and kept shouting and shouting.

7

One side screamed, "Standing up!"

The other side shrieked, "Lying down!"

9

"Standing Up!"

"Lying **DOWN!**"

"Standing Up!"

"Lying **DOWN!**"

The two sides yelled and yelled. They argued all through the day.

14

They argued all through the night.

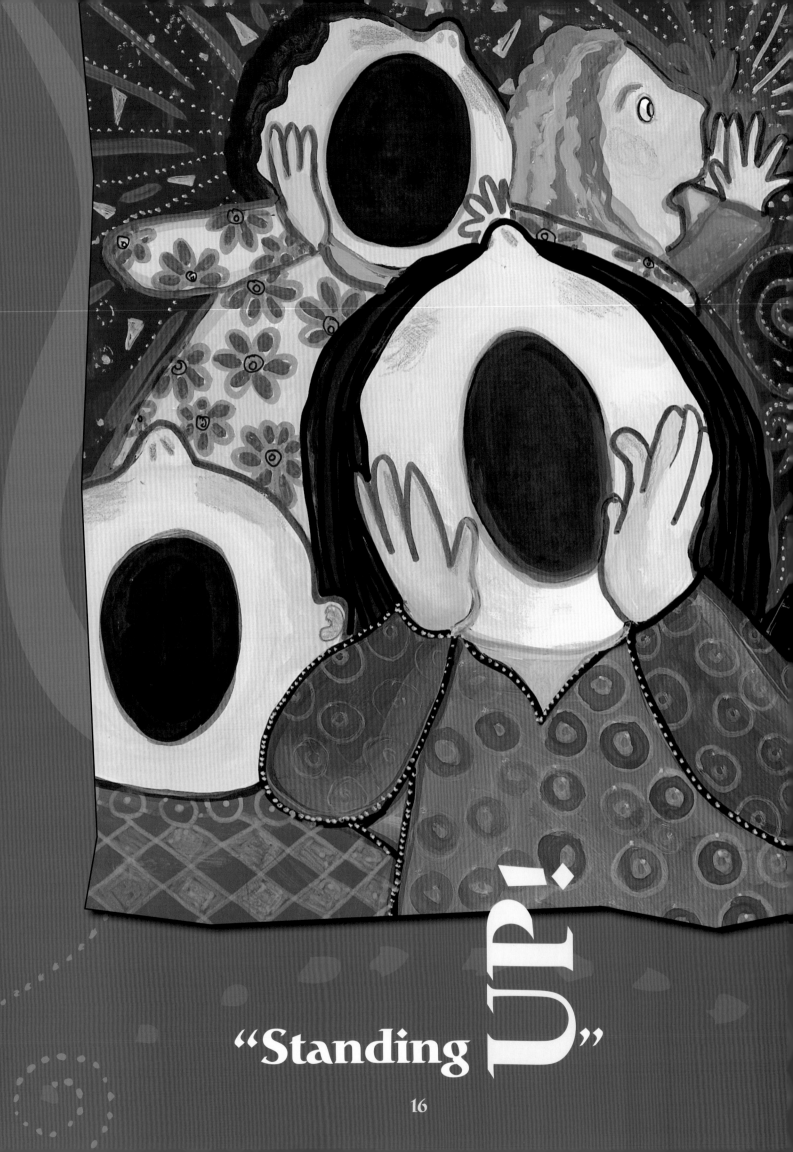

"Standing UP!"

"Lying **DOWN!**"

What were the people to do? They decided to ask the rabbi of the town.
The rabbi turned his head to one side and listened.

The rabbi turned his head to the other side and listened.

He turned to look at the buildings in the town. None of them had a mezuzah on the doorway.

"What are we to do?" the townspeople asked the rabbi. "Shall we put the mezuzah standing up or lying down?"

To the people who believed that the mezuzah should be standing up, the rabbi said, "You are right."

To the people who believed that the mezuzah should be lying down, the rabbi said, "You are right."

23

The townspeople were puzzled. "Rabbi, how can we all be right? We can't have the mezuzah standing up and lying down at the same time."

The rabbi smiled, "You are right again."

"Very funny, Rabbi," both sides agreed.

But the rabbi wasn't laughing. "You haven't read the instructions very carefully. The very first word on the mezuzah's special paper is

Listen, *Shema.*

Listen to one another. You must put the mezuzah on the doorway so that it is standing up—a little—and lying down—a little."

25

The people who wanted the mezuzah standing up listened to the people who wanted it lying down and said, "Well, if we slant the mezuzah, it will almost be standing up."

The people who wanted the mezuzah lying down listened to the people who wanted it standing up and said, "Well, if we slant the mezuzah, it will almost be lying down."

Both sides liked the rabbi's idea.

The people stopped shouting.
They stopped arguing.
They stopped yelling.
They listened.

They put up the mezuzahs. The people lived in many different kinds of homes, but they were one people. It is just like the *Shema* tells us,

"God is One."

"And that is how," Annie's grandmother said, "it has been ever since. When we place the mezuzah on our doorway, it is not standing up and it is not lying down. It is leaning into our home, just the way it should be."

"When we enter our home and we see the leaning mezuzah, we remember," she said softly. "We stop shouting. We stop arguing. We stop yelling at each other.

We listen.
We are one."